J 793.8 Eld
Eldin, P.
Make your own magic tricks.
Caledon Public Library
FEB 2017   3582

PRICE: $6.57 (3582/01   )

Make Your Own Magic Tricks

Peter Eldin   Alfredo Belli

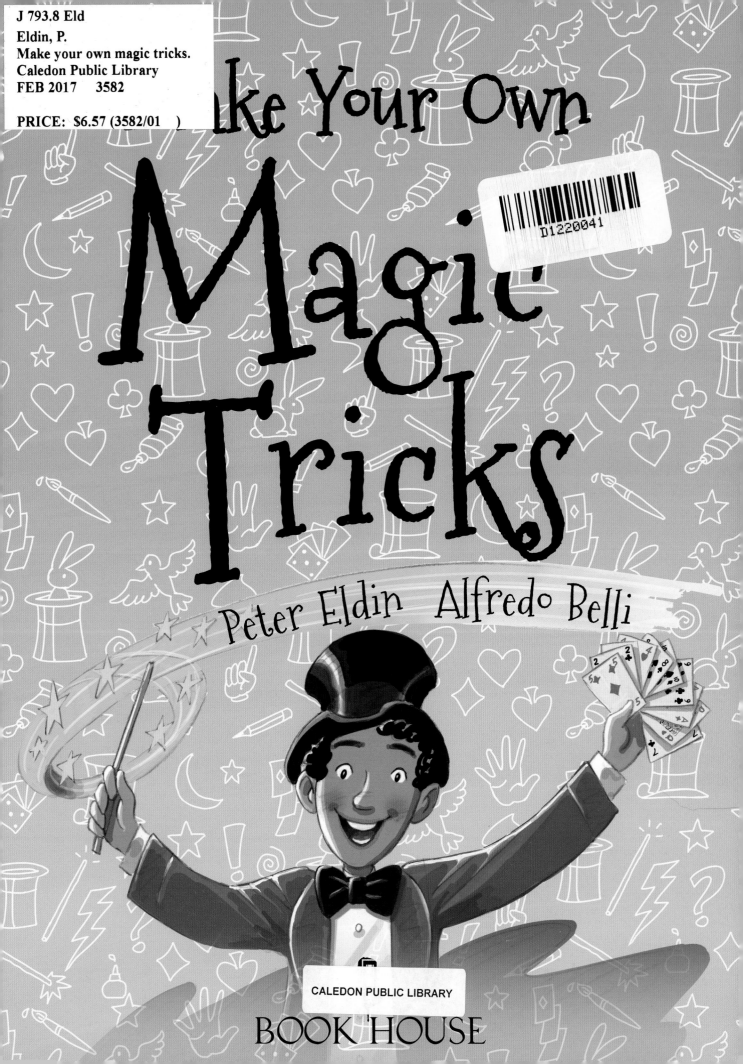

CALEDON PUBLIC LIBRARY

BOOK HOUSE

Rules of Magic

- Practise each trick well before you perform it.

- Where a trick is set up for a right-handed person and you are left-handed - just change hands.

- Never repeat a trick even if someone asks you to do it again.

- **Never** tell anyone how a trick is done.

- If a trick needs some extra preparation - do this secretly.

- Before you perform a trick, work out and practise what you plan to say. Write out your script and learn it thoroughly to present your 'act' with confidence.

- Enjoy your magic. If you don't enjoy it, you can't expect your audience to enjoy it.

What you'll need

You do not need any special equipment to do magic. All the projects in this book can be done with items you will have at home or which are easily obtainable. These include: thin card, paper, envelopes, glue, pens, crayons, tracing paper, scissors, dowelling, paint, toothpicks, coins, ribbons and handkerchiefs.

Add some of the stickers to your tricks to make them look more magical and mysterious.

Make a magic wand

You will need:
- Wooden dowelling (about 25 cm long)
- Black paint
- White paint

Paint the middle part of the dowelling black, and the ends white. This is a traditional wand but you can make yours more colourful if you wish. You could use glitter paint to make your wand sparkle.

Make a mini wand

You will need:
- Unsharpened pencil
- White paper or thin card
- Black paint or felt-tip pen
- Glue

Glue white paper around the unsharpened pencil. Colour the middle part black. You now have a mini wand you can use for your tricks.

A magic wand is the magician's traditional symbol of power. Wave it in the air or tap objects with it 'to make the magic work'.

Time will tell

T ricks that use familiar
props such as a clock let
you make magic out of the
ordinary and everyday.

You will need:
- Press-out Clock dial (p. 17)
  (or a real clock or watch)
- Magic wand

To do the trick:

1. Show one of your audience the watch dial. Ask them to think of any number on the dial. Then they must start counting from the number above the one thought of, as you tap the dial with your magic wand. For example, if they thought of 6, they start counting '7, 8, 9...'

The audience member is to count to 20 and then call 'stop'. Believe it or not, but the wand will now be pointing to the very number thought of in the first place.

2. To do this you make seven taps at random. The eighth tap must be on the number 12.

Now tap the numbers, one at a time, anti clockwise around the dial.

When the spectator has counted 20 taps your wand will be pointing at the chosen number!

Star turn

This simple card trick is easy to prepare, but it can make a big impact on your audience. You must practise it repeatedly so that you can perform it quickly and smoothly.

Practise in front of a mirror so you can see what it looks like before you try it out on your friends.

You will need:
- A piece of card measuring about 10 cm x 12 cm
- Seven star stickers (from pages 9, 12, 14-15) - stick two stars on one side of the card and five stars on the other, as shown.

To do the trick:

1. Hold up the side of the card with two stars on it, covering the bottom star with your fingers.
Say 'Side one has one star.'

2. Hold up the other side, but this time place your fingers over the middle star.
Say 'Side two has four stars.'

3. Show the first side again, but put your fingers over the blank space at the bottom.
Say 'Side three has three stars.'

4. Show the other side again with your fingers covering the blank space.
Say 'And side four has six stars.'

Multiplying money

W ouldn't it be handy if we could magically increase our money? This magic trick will make it seem as if that is exactly what you can do!

You will need:
- Coin tray template (p. 32)
- Scissors
- Glue
- Some coins

Secret preparation:

1

1. Press out the 'coin tray' template on page 32.

2

2. Fold in both side flaps and add glue to them.

3. Fold the top section down over the glued flaps and press firmly. Once the glue has dried, decorate the tray with magic shapes or add some stickers to it.

3

4. Put a few coins inside the 'secret' pocket of the tray. You are now ready to do the trick.

4

To do the trick:

1. Hold out the tray with some coins on top of it.

2. Ask someone to add up the value of the coins.

3. You now tip the coins from the tray onto their hands.

4. The hidden coins will pour out at the same time.

5. Now ask the spectator to count the money again. It's increased in value! How did you do that?

You will choose

If you master this trick, your friends will be amazed at your mind-reading abilities.

You will need:

- Stickers showing a magic wand, a top hat and a fan of cards
- An envelope (p. 17)
- Four pieces of card that fit inside the envelope
- Pencil, crayon or pen
- Scissors

Secret preparation:

1. Make up the envelope by gluing together the template on page 17.

1

2. Add a sticker to three of the cards.

2

3. On the fourth card write: "you will choose the **top hat**".

On the front of the envelope write: "you will choose the **playing cards** picture".

On the back of the **magic wand** card write: "I knew you would choose this one".

Place all four cards into the envelope and put it in your pocket.

3

To do the trick:

1. Pick up the envelope, but be careful not to let anyone see what is written on the front of it.

2. Take out the three sticker cards only. Keep the remaining card and message concealed in the envelope so no one can see it.

3. Place the three picture cards on the table. Do not let anyone touch the cards or they may see the writing on the back of the 'magic wand' card.

4. Ask someone to pick one of the three stickered cards. If they choose the '**playing cards**' one, you will turn over the envelope to reveal the message that you knew this would be their choice.
If the '**top hat**' card is chosen, take the concealed card from the envelope and reveal its message (keep the envelope face down so the writing on the front is not visible).
If the '**magic wand**' card is chosen, just turn it over to reveal the message written there.

Make sure you keep all the written messages hidden until you know which card has been chosen. As soon as the trick is over, gather all the cards and put them back in the envelope before anyone can examine them.

Coin go

You will need:

- Coin
- Handkerchief
- Small elastic band

With this trick, you can make a friend's money disappear. Fortunately for them, it's only temporary!

To do the trick:

1. Hide the elastic band in your right hand and spread the handkerchief over it. Quickly arrange the elastic band over your fingers, as shown. Hold up the coin in your left hand before placing it on the centre of the handkerchief.

1

2. Push the coin down so it goes through the middle of the concealed elastic band.

2

3. Now shake out the handkerchief. The coin will appear to have vanished but it is really hidden in the little pocket formed by the elastic band.

3

26

Coloured thoughts

Most tricks should never be repeated, but this one is an exception. The more times you guess correctly, the more mystified your friends will be!

You will need:
- Mixed box of coloured wax crayons

To do the trick:

1. Turn away from your audience. Ask someone to pick any coloured crayon out of the box and hand it to you behind your back.

2. Now turn to your audience with your hands still behind your back. Carefully scrape the surface of the crayon with one of your fingernails. Bring this hand up to your head as if concentrating. This gives you time to look at your fingernail to identify the colour.

3. Finally, make your dramatic announcement of the chosen colour. Bring the crayon forward, show it to the audience, and place it back in the box.

Cruel cut

This is a miniature, table-top version of the famous magic trick: 'saw the lady in half'.

You will need:
- Tube template (p. 30)
- Card
- Scissors
- Figure template (p. 30)
- Paints or crayons

To do the trick:

1. Show the audience the tube and the figure templates. **Don't** let anyone see the slits in the tube.

2. Slide the figure into the tube. The secret is to push the figure out of the first slit at the back and then in through the second slit again.

3. Now cut the tube in half. Secretly, you must slide the lower blade of the scissors in between the figure and the tube. Cut the envelope in two but pull out the figure, still in one piece - magic!

Secret preparation:

Press out the tube template. Cut the two slits in the back of the tube. Fold over the flap, add glue and stick it to the other edge. Draw stars or add some stickers to decorate the tube.
Press out the figure template and colour in her hair, face and clothing.

Knotted!

This trick can be performed anywhere, at any time, and comes with a twist in its tale.

You will need:
- Two coloured handkerchiefs or scarves
- Small elastic band

To do the trick:

1. Try to conceal the elastic band over your fingers by initially holding both handkerchiefs in this hand.

2. Now hold up the handkerchiefs to the audience, one in each hand.

3. Quickly take both handkerchiefs in one hand and secretly slip the elastic band over both of them.

4. Throw the handkerchiefs into the air. Catch one of them as they fall and it will seem that they are knotted together by magic.

33

Acrobatic band

You will need:
- Elastic band

A quick trick like this is ideal when performing magic at a party, where people's attention spans are limited.

To do the trick:

1. Put the elastic band over the first two fingers of your left hand. Pull the band with your other hand to prove to your audience that it really is around the fingers.

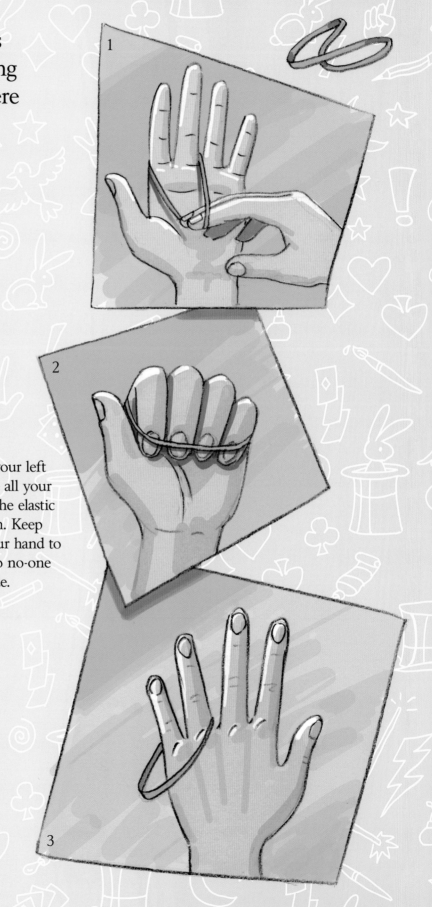

2. Now close your left hand and place all your fingers under the elastic band, as shown. Keep the back of your hand to the audience so no-one can see this side.

3. Now quickly open your left hand again and the band will then jump across to the third and fourth fingers. It will look as if the elastic band has travelled right through your fingers!

This trick is simple but needs lots of practice.

Sleight of hand

You will need:
- Coin

Magic tricks commonly involve sleight of hand. Practice makes perfect. These kind of tricks are simple but rely on fast, confident action.

1

2

3

4

5

To do the trick:

1. Hold a coin between the thumb and first finger of your left hand.

2. Bring your right hand over so the thumb goes under the coin and the fingers go over it, hiding it from view.

3. Close your right hand as if you are taking the coin. At the same time let the coin drop into the palm of your left hand.

4. Raise your clasped right hand as if it is holding the coin.

5. Slowly open your right hand - the coin has vanished!

This is a good way to make almost any small object seem to disappear.

Clipped

This trick creates the illusion that two inanimate paper clips have been magically brought to life.

You will need:
- Two paper clips
- A bank note

To do the trick:

1. First borrow a bank note from someone in the audience.

2. Hold up the two paper clips for everyone to see. Fold the bank note into an 's' shape, as shown.

3. Place the paper clips on the note. One clip goes over the back two layers of paper on your left. The other goes on the front two layers of the note on your right.

4. Pulling briskly on each end of the note will make the clips fly off, linked together!

Thumb fun

Optical illusions can make for great magic. This trick makes it look as if you can remove your left thumb and then put it back again!

To do the trick:

1. Hold your left hand in front of you with the palm facing your stomach. Bring your right hand over.

2. Place your right index finger on the knuckle of your left thumb. At the same time bend the left thumb downwards and move your right-hand thumb across to touch it.

3. Lift your right fingers up so that what the audience sees is your left thumb and right thumb with your index finger covering the gap. It should look as if it is just your left thumb they are seeing.

4. Now slide your right hand and thumb to the right and back again. Only perform this trick when your audience is directly in front of you so they can't see what you're doing.

37

Torn and restored

Baffle your audience by appearing to tear up and then restore a strip of paper.

You will need:
- Two strips of paper, 16 cm x 4 cm
- Glue

Secret preparation:

- Fold one strip of paper, concertina fashion, until it is quite small.
- Glue this folded strip onto the end of the other strip.
- Let the glue dry before putting the strips in your pocket.

To do the trick:

1. Take the long paper strip from your pocket and hold it up between your hands. Keep the folded concertina strip hidden from view.

1

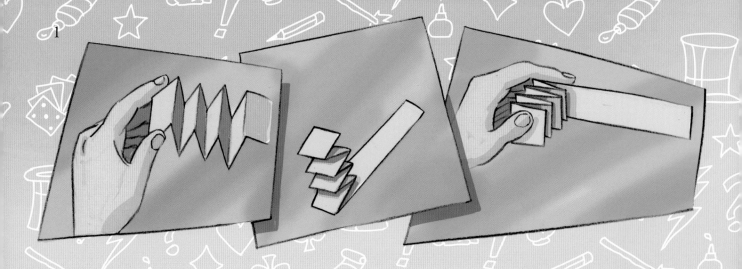

2. Hold the long strip up, give a quick tug and tear it in half.

3. Put one half on top of the other. Keep tearing the strips in half like this until they are the same size as the hidden folded strip.

4. Hold all the pieces in your right hand and wave your left hand over them in a 'magic' manner. Now change hands but turn the pieces over as you do so.

5. The concertina folded strip is now in front of all the torn pieces. Pull the folded strip open but keep the torn pieces hidden behind it.

6. Pause for a moment with the paper held between your hands. It looks as if you have restored the paper into one piece by magic.
Bow to the audience as you put the strip and all the torn pieces safely away in your pocket.

Sticky wand

This is a good trick to know because you can do it either with a magic wand or with almost anything else: a pencil, a stick, or even a drinking straw!

You will need:
- Magic wand
- Two hands

To do the trick:

1. First hold the wand up to show your audience. Then clasp your hands together so that the middle finger of the right hand is not part of the interweaving. From the front, your hands appear to be clasped.

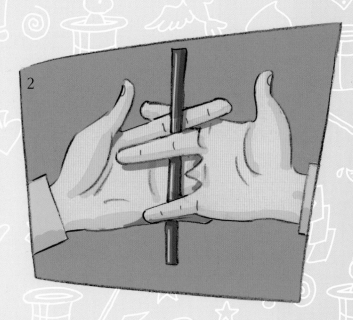

2. Practise this until you can do it without thinking, as if you really are linking your fingers together. Take the wand and position it behind the middle finger.

3. From the front the wand appears to be glued to your hand. To prove that no glue is used unclasp your hands and give the wand to someone else to try.

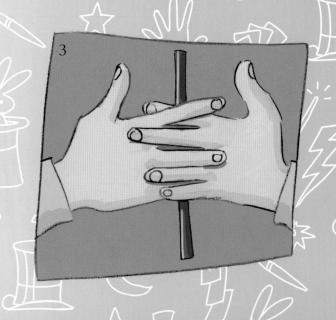

Going through

U sually waving a magic wand makes other things disappear, but in this trick it's the wand itself that vanishes.

You will need:
• Handkerchief
• Mini wand

To do the trick:

1. Lay the handkerchief on the table with the wand on top.

2. Take the handkerchief corner nearest to you and fold it up over the wand and slightly beyond the corner furthest from you.

3. Roll the centre of the handkerchief around the wand. Keep rolling until you see one of the corners.

4. Pull the two corners apart to open out the handkerchief. The wand seems to have vanished. Lift up the handkerchief and show the wand on the table. It must have passed right through the handkerchief!

41

Ribbon repair

This deceptively simple trick involves making your audience believe that you have magically repaired a piece of ribbon that has been cut in two.

You will need:
- Ribbon (about 30 cm long)
- Scissors
- Needle
- Thread (same colour as the ribbon)

Secret preparation:

Cut 8 centimetres from the end of the ribbon and sew it on to the middle of the long piece.

Use only one stitch at each end of the small piece of ribbon as you need to pretend to break it off when you do the trick.

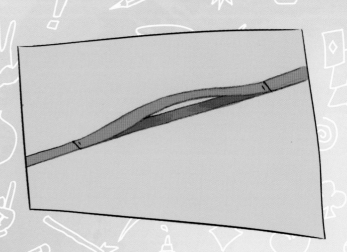

To do the trick:

1. Hold up the ribbon to show the audience, making sure the extra piece in the middle is not seen.
Fold the ribbon in half and hold the centre of it in your left hand (make sure the short piece is uppermost as shown above).

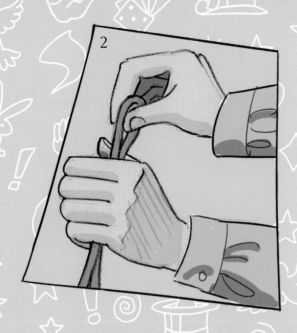

2. Use your right hand to pull the middle of the ribbon out of your left fist. Actually it is the short, extra piece that you have lifted into view. The long piece of ribbon stays hidden in your left fist.

3. The picture on the right shows how the ribbon would look if you could see through the hand. Now take the scissors and cut through the middle of this extra piece to look as if you have cut the ribbon in two.

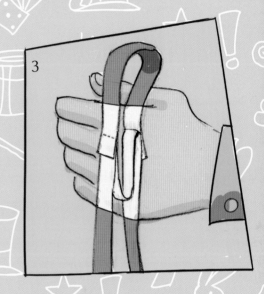

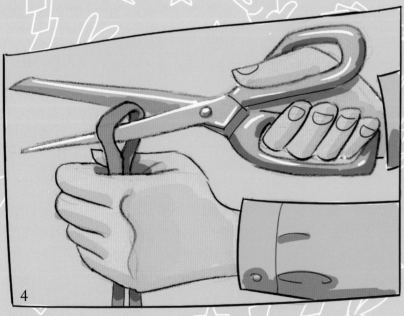

4. Now cut off the ends of the small piece as if you are just trimming it - actually you are removing the short piece.

5. Finally pull at what is left of the short ribbon so it comes away from the longer piece.
Your audience will think you are just neatening the ends of the ribbon in your left hand.
Surprise them by revealing the whole ribbon completely restored!

That's torn it

You will need:
- Paper
- Coin

Y ou don't need lots of elaborate equipment to put on a magic show. This trick can be performed with two items that can be found anywhere.

To do the trick:

1. Place the coin on a piece of paper a little below the centre.

2. Fold the bottom edge of the paper up over the coin. Then fold both sides in.

3. It now looks as if the coin is sealed in but, in fact the top edge is open.

4. Tap the package with your magic wand to prove the coin is still there.

5. At the same time, casually turn the package upside down so the open edge is at the bottom. Allow the coin to slide out into your hand, unseen. Keep the coin hidden in your hand and tear up the paper. The coin appears to have vanished!

5

Hidden numbers

I mpress your audience with this trick that secretly uses simple mathematics to conjure up a seemingly impossible answer.

You will need:
* Three dice (or use the dice template on p. 19)
* Some mental arithmetic

To do the trick:

1. Hand the three dice to someone in your audience. Turn your back and ask them to throw the dice and then stack them, one on top of the other.

2. Tell your audience that five sides of the dice are now hidden from view. It is impossible for anyone to know what these numbers would add up to - without moving the dice.

3. Then all you have to do is look at the number on top of the stack. Subtract that number from 21 to find the total of all the 'hidden' numbers.

In the meantime...'act out' your best impression of magical powers - then reveal the answer!

A spectacular production

You will need:
- Two sheets of card
- Paper clips
- Small elastic band
- Coloured ribbon (or different coloured ribbons sewn together)

Most of the work required to perform this trick is at the preparation stages. If you take the time to get your equipment ready, it should be a great success.

Secret preparation:

Fold each sheet of card into a tube. Hold the edges together with paper clips (or glue them together). One tube must be thinner than the other. Add some stickers to both tubes to make them look magical.

Roll up the ribbon and use the elastic band to hold the roll together. Bend one of the paperclips into a hook shape. Tie one end of the ribbon to the paperclip hook.
Use the hook to hang the rolled up ribbon inside the thinner tube. Put both tubes on your table ready for your show.

To do the trick:

1. Hold up the large tube and show it to your audience. Allow everyone to see right through it.

2. Now take the thinner tube, drop it through the large tube and catch it. This secretly transfers the ribbons into the large tube.

3. Hold up the thinner tube to show to the audience and put it back on your table.

4. Then place the large tube over the thinner tube. Reach into the top of the tubes, pull the elastic band from the ribbons and then slowly pull out the long length of coloured ribbon - magic!

47

Put on a show

When you are confident about your magic skills you might like to put on a special show for your family and friends. This needs some planning so think carefully about what you are going to do.

Here are some tips:

- Grab your audience's attention - start with a good, quick trick.
- Longer tricks should go in the middle of your act.
- Finish with your best trick.
- Don't make your act too long - 15 minutes is enough.
- Know what's needed for each trick and where to find it in your box.
- Know where to return the things used for each trick.
- Smile! Convince your audience of your magician's skills.

The magic box:

It is a good idea to put everything you need for your show in a large cardboard box. You can paint it or cover it with coloured paper. Draw some magic symbols on the box or add some of the stickers from this book to make it look more impressive.